A Child's Book of
Prayers and Blessings

For Michael and his wife, Yvette, who have
blessed our family with twins, Victoria and
Isabel. My prayer is that this book will be
loved by my granddaughters and their parents.
I pray this book will be loved by all young
readers and parents, and help them to know
how special they are, as God created us all.

—D. J.

For Ava, Zyanya, and David III
Welcome to our big beautiful world

—S. S.

SIMON & SCHUSTER BOOKS FOR YOUNG READERS • An imprint of Simon & Schuster Children's
Publishing Division • 1230 Avenue of the Americas, New York, New York 10020 • Text copyright © 2017 by Deloris
Jordan • Illustrations copyright © 2017 by Shadra Strickland • All rights reserved, including the right of reproduction in whole or in part
in any form. • SIMON & SCHUSTER BOOKS FOR YOUNG READERS is a trademark of Simon & Schuster, Inc. • For information about special
discounts for bulk purchases, please contact Simon & Schuster Special Sales at 1-866-506-1949 or business@simonandschuster.com. • The Simon & Schuster
Speakers Bureau can bring authors to your live event. For more information or to book an event, contact the Simon & Schuster Speakers Bureau at 1-866-248-3049 or visit our
website at www.simonspeakers.com. • Book design by Laurent Linn • The text for this book is set in Arrus BT Std. • The illustrations for this book were created using a hand
printed reduction linoleum printmaking technique. • Manufactured in China • 0717 SCP • First Edition • 10 9 8 7 6 5 4 3 2 1 • Library of Congress Cataloging-in-Publication
Data • Jordan, Deloris. • A child's book of prayers and blessings / Deloris Jordan : illustrated by Shadra Strickland.—1st ed. • p. cm. • Includes authors and sources. •
ISBN 978-1-4169-9550-0 (alk. paper) • 1. Children—Prayers and devotions. I. Strickland, Shadra, ill. II. Title. • BV265.J87 2010 • 242'.62—dc22 • 2010029663

A Child's Book of Prayers and Blessings

From Faiths and Cultures Around the World

Deloris Jordan

ARTWORK BY Shadra Strickland

A Paula Wiseman Book

SIMON & SCHUSTER BOOKS FOR YOUNG READERS

New York London Toronto Sydney New Delhi

Child's Blessing

May God bless you and watch over you.
May God shine His face toward you and show you favor.
May God look on you with favor and grant you peace.

—OLD TESTAMENT

A Child's Prayer for Morning

Now before I run to play,
Let me not forget to pray
To God, who kept me through the night
And waked me with the morning light.
Help me, Lord, to love thee more
Than I ever loved before,
In my work and in my play
Be thou with me through the day.
Amen.

—TRADITIONAL

All Things Bright and Beautiful

All things bright and beautiful,
All creatures great and small,
All things wise and wonderful:
The Lord God made them all.

Each little flower that opens,
Each little bird that sings,
He made their glowing colors,
He made their tiny wings.

The purple headed mountains,
The river running by,
The sunset and the morning
That brightens up the sky.

The cold wind in the winter,
The pleasant summer sun,
The ripe fruits in the garden,
He made them every one.

All things bright and beautiful,
All creatures great and small,
All things wise and wonderful:
The Lord God made them all.

The tall trees in the greenwood,
The meadows where we play,
The rushes by the water,
To gather every day.

All things bright and beautiful,
All creatures great and small,
All things wise and wonderful:
The Lord God made them all.

He gave us eyes to see them,
And lips that we might tell
How great is God Almighty,
Who has made all things well.

All things bright and beautiful,
All creatures great and small,
All things wise and wonderful:
The Lord God made them all.

—CECIL F. ALEXANDER

Ancient Tibetan Buddhist Blessing

May you be filled with loving kindness.
May you be well.
May you be peaceful and at ease.
May you be happy.

—TRADITIONAL

Earth and Sky

The earth is big and fat and round,
I love the sky, the sea, and the ground,
I love the birds and dogs and sheep,
And all the animals that fall asleep,
I love the flowers and rocks and trees,
I love the earth, and it loves me.

—TRADITIONAL

He's Got the Whole World in His Hands

He's got the whole world in His hands.
He's got the big round world in His hands.
He's got the whole round world in His hands.

He's got the wind and the rain . . .

He's got the little baby . . .

He's got you and me, sister . . .

He's got you and me, brother . . .

—AMERICAN SPIRITUAL

Golden Light

Golden Light, shining bright,
Always teach me what is right.
Teach me to speak with kindness and care.
Teach me to be willing to share.
Teach me to remember, when playing with others,
That all of us are world sisters and brothers.
Golden Light, shining bright,
Keep our world family safe every night.

—TRADITIONAL

Remembrance of God

Bismillah
In the name of God
Alhamdulillah
Thanks be to God
Subhanallah
Glory is from God
Mashallah
As God wishes
Inshallah
If God wills

—MUSLIM WORDS OF PRAYER

Here's the Church

Here's the church, and here's the steeple.
Open the doors and see all the people.
Here's the parson going upstairs,
And here he is saying his prayers.

—TRADITIONAL

Navajo Song

It is lovely indeed, it is lovely indeed.
I, I am the spirit within the earth . . .
The feet of the earth are my feet . . .
The legs of the earth are my legs . . .
The bodily strength of the earth is my strength . . .
The thoughts of the earth are my thoughts . . .
The voice of the earth is my voice . . .
The feather of the earth is my feather . . .
All that belongs to the earth belongs to me . . .
All that surrounds the earth surrounds me . . .
I, I am the sacred words of the earth . . .
It is lovely indeed, it is lovely indeed.

—NATIVE AMERICAN

Kumbaya

Kumbaya, my Lord, kumbaya
Kumbaya, my Lord, kumbaya
Kumbaya, my Lord, kumbaya
Oh Lord, kumbaya

Someone's singing, Lord, kumbaya
Someone's singing, Lord, kumbaya
Someone's singing, Lord, kumbaya
Oh Lord, kumbaya

Someone's laughing, Lord, kumbaya
Someone's laughing, Lord, kumbaya
Someone's laughing, Lord, kumbaya
Oh Lord, kumbaya

Someone's crying, Lord, kumbaya
Someone's crying, Lord, kumbaya
Someone's crying, Lord, kumbaya
Oh Lord, kumbaya

Someone's praying, Lord, kumbaya
Someone's praying, Lord, kumbaya
Someone's praying, Lord, kumbaya
Oh Lord, kumbaya

  Someone's sleeping, Lord, kumbaya
  Someone's sleeping, Lord, kumbaya
  Someone's sleeping, Lord, kumbaya
  Oh Lord, kumbaya
  Oh Lord, kumbaya

—AMERICAN SPIRITUAL

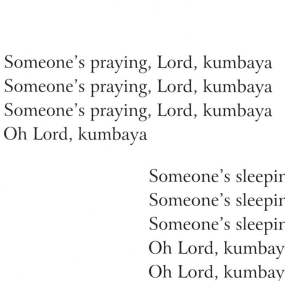

God, Hear My Prayer

God, in heaven, hear my prayer,
Keep me in your loving care.
Be my guide in all I do,
Bless all those who love me too.

—TRADITIONAL

Child's Prayer

Dear God most high, hear and bless
The beasts and singing birds;
And guard with tenderness
Small things that have no words.

—TRADITIONAL

Michael, Row the Boat Ashore

Michael, row the boat ashore,
Hallelujah!
Then you'll hear the trumpet blow,
Hallelujah!

Then you'll hear the trumpet sound,
Hallelujah!
Trumpet sound the world around,
Hallelujah!

Trumpet sound the jubilee,
Hallelujah!
Trumpet sound for you and me,
Hallelujah!

—AMERICAN SPIRITUAL

This Little Light of Mine

This little light of mine,
I'm going to let it shine.
Oh, this little light of mine,
I'm going to let it shine,
Hallelujah.
This little light of mine,
I'm going to let it shine.
Let it shine, let it shine, let it shine.

Ev'ry where I go,
I'm going to let it shine.
Oh, ev'ry where I go,
I'm going to let it shine,
Hallelujah.
Ev'ry where I go,
I'm going to let it shine.
Let it shine, let it shine, let it shine.

All in my house,
I'm going to let it shine.
Oh, all in my house,
I'm going to let it shine,
Hallelujah.
All in my house,
I'm going to let it shine.
Let it shine, let it shine, let it shine.

I'm not going to make it shine,
I'm just going to let it shine.
I'm not going to make it shine,
I'm just going to let it shine,
Hallelujah.
I'm not going to make it shine,
I'm just going to let it shine.
Let it shine, let it shine, let it shine.

Out in the dark,
I'm going to let it shine.
Oh, out in the dark,
I'm going to let it shine,
Hallelujah.
Out in the dark,
I'm going to let it shine.
Let it shine, let it shine, let it shine.

—AVIS BURGESON CHRISTIANSEN

Child's Mealtime Blessing

Thank you for the world so sweet,
Thank you for the food we eat.
Thank you for the birds that sing,
Thank you God for everything.

—TRADITIONAL

For Happy Hearts

We thank thee, Lord, for happy hearts,
For rain and sunny weather.
We thank thee, Lord, for this our food,
And that we are together.

—TRADITIONAL

Now I Lay Me Down to Sleep

Now I lay me down to sleep,
I pray the Lord my soul to keep:
May God guard me through the night
And wake me with the morning light.
Amen.

—JOSEPH ADDISON

Prayer for a Child

Bless this milk and bless this bread.
Bless this soft and waiting bed
Where I presently shall be
Wrapped in sweet security.
Through the darkness, through the night
Let no danger come to fright
My sleep till morning once again
Beckons at the window pane.
Bless the toys whose shapes I know,
The shoes that take me to and fro
Up and down and everywhere.

—RACHEL FIELD

Children's Bedtime Prayer

Bless me Lord, this night I pray,
Keep me safe till dawn of day,
Bless my mother and my father,
Bless my sister and my brother,
Bless each little girl and boy,
Bless them all for heavenly joy.
Amen.

—TRADITIONAL

Angel Blessing at Bedtime

Angels bless and angels keep
Angels guard me while I sleep
Bless my heart and bless my home
Bless my spirit as I roam
Guide and guard me through the night
And wake me with the morning's light.
Amen.

—TRADITIONAL

Authors and Sources

A Child's Prayer for Morning
Traditional. Author unknown. Public domain.

All Things Bright and Beautiful
Anglican hymn by Cecil F. Alexander. From *Hymns for Little Children*, 1848. Public domain.

Ancient Tibetan Buddhist Blessing
Traditional. Author unknown. Public domain.

Angel Blessing at Bedtime
Traditional. Author unknown. Public domain.

Children's Bedtime Prayer
Traditional. Author unknown. Public domain.

Child's Blessing
English translation taken from Aaron's blessing in the Old Testament, Numbers 6:22–27. This is a transliteration of the Hebrew:
Ye'varech'echa Adonoy ve'yish'merecha.
Yaerr Adonoy panav eilecha viy-chuneka.
Yisah Adonoy panav eilecha, ve'yasem lecha shalom.
Traditionally used as a Friday blessing prior to the Sabbath.

Child's Mealtime Blessing
Traditional. Author unknown. Public domain.

Child's Prayer
Traditional. Author unknown. Public domain.

Earth and Sky
Traditional. Author unknown. Public domain.

For Happy Hearts
Traditional. Author unknown. Public domain.

God, Hear My Prayer
Traditional. Author unknown. Public domain.

Golden Light
Traditional. Author unknown. Public domain.

Here's the Church
Traditional nursery finger rhyme. Can be said with interlocked hands that inverted show people in church. Traditional. Author unknown. Public domain.

He's Got the Whole World in His Hands
Traditional American spiritual. First published in the paperbound hymnal *Spirituals Triumphant, Old and New* in 1927. Public domain.

Kumbaya
American spiritual song first recorded in 1927 by Robert Winslow Gordon. The English language translation of "Kumbaya" is "Come by here." Author and composer unknown. Public domain.

Michael, Row the Boat Ashore
American Spiritual. The song was first published in *Slave Songs of the United States* in 1867 by William Francis Allen, Charles Pickard Ware, and Lucy McKim Garrison. Public domain.

Navajo Song
Traditional Native American Navajo song. Author unknown. Public domain.

Now I Lay Me Down to Sleep
Classic children's bedtime prayer from the eighteenth century. Adapted from Joseph Addison's *The Spectator*, 1711. Public domain.

Prayer for a Child
Rachel Field. Excerpt first published in 1941 as "The Baby's Prayer," and later published as "Prayer for a Child," illustrated by Elizabeth Orton Jones. Used by permission of Simon & Schuster Children's Publishing.

Remembrance of God
Islamic prayer always said in Arabic. Public domain.

This Little Light of Mine
From "This Little Light of Mine." American gospel song with lyrics by Avis Burgeson Christiansen (1895–1985) and music by composer and Harry Dixon Loes (1892–1965). Written on or around 1920. Public domain.